I0445488

BAREBACK MAID

DIRTY BILLIONAIRE BOSS

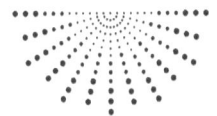

TALA MELTON

plicit Press
Erotica Fiction

GET NAUGHTY UPDATES

Click here or Visit
TalaMelton.com
for more Naughty Maid Stories

CHAPTER ONE

*L*uke White, late 40s, was the first of the six executives to throw a lustful eye at Raquel. It had been about two hours since the private plane had taken off from New York, headed for Paris. Over the Atlantic, everyone had settled into the flight, everyone except Raquel, that is, who shouldn't have been on this flight in the first place.

"Thanks for doing this so last minute," billionaire Dean said, as he took a drink from her.

"No problem, Sir," she answered her boss, before passing out the other drinks.

"You seem uncomfortable," Luke said, his fingers lingering ever so slightly too long on Raquel's hand as he took his drink from her. She looked instinctively at Dean.

"I'm fine," she said, "I just don't like flying!"

She made her escape to the back of the plane and sat in her seat after securing her tray in place. She was facing the seven men who had their backs to her in varying degrees. The aircraft was designed this way so that the hostess could anticipate the needs of the guests without being intrusive.

Raquel just appreciated that she was, for the most part, out of view, out of view to everyone except Luke, that is, who kept turning his head 180 degrees so that he was looking directly at her.

Raquel was as confident as she was beautiful, though, so this didn't bother her. Her blonde hair was high on her head in a neat bun. She used her compact to perfect her already perfect makeup, pretending not to notice Luke's incessant stares. He really was making no secret of the fact that he was ogling at her.

Suddenly the pilot's voice came over the intercom, clear as crystal. The more frequent flyers were undisturbed by the announcement, but two words rang loudly in Raquel's head: *EMERGENCY LANDING!*

The pilot proceeded to explain something about the *warning light malfunctioning, and just to be on the safe side, they would turn back towards Atlanta since there wasn't an opportunity to land back at JFK.* It added a few hours to the flight but, *better safe than sorry.*

The landing wasn't as dramatic as Raquel had anticipated. In fact, she wasn't even aware that they had already taxied into a hanger and that there were already mechanics hard at work to fix whatever the problem was.

"Raquel..." Luke said, lifting his glass. She undid her seatbelt and got to her feet. She was very short, even for the inside of the small plane. Standing at just 5"2, she made her way to the gentlemen, still seated, pushing her trolley this time just so that she could give them what they wanted to drink. Five of them took soft drinks from her and exited the aircraft. They were not going to sit around doing nothing. Apparently, doing nothing outside the plane was more appealing.

She turned to Dean, who was face deep in paperwork already. "Would you like something to drink, Sir," she asked

Dean, who really looked busy. He scanned the sentence he was reading before looking up.

"Yes, I'll have a whiskey, straight up, no ice..." As she poured him the drink, his eyes scanned her with the same scrutiny as he had just perused the document. "It looks good on you, the uniform..." he said, taking the glass from her.

"That it does," Luke chimed in unnecessarily.

"Thank you, Sir," she said to Dean only.

"You ever think of, Uhm, *you know*, with this one?" Luke asked Dean when Raquel was back in her seat, although he asked the question so loudly that he didn't need to wait for her to be *'out of earshot!'*

Dean looked at her; she looked at him. Raquel was clearly also curious as to what the answer to this particular question would be. "I don't think she'd let me," he answered candidly, still looking at Raquel. She smiled a little and then looked away.

"Wouldn't let you? Why not?" Luke pressed.

"Because I'm old, Luke. We're old!"

Raquel laughed louder than she intended, both Luke and Dean looking at her now.

"Speak for yourself..." Luke said, and he got up and left the aircraft, just to stretch his legs. He winked at Raquel on his way out, and she winked back before she could catch herself.

Alone now with Dean, she thought of his answer. She wondered what, if anything, could have given him the impression that she wouldn't sleep with him, that he was old. Yes, he was *older*, but that wasn't a bad thing. Not for him, at least. He looked incredible, evidence of a healthy lifestyle written on his face and his physique. Raquel found herself staring at Dean now, the way Luke had stared at her earlier.

"Can I get you anything else," she asked when he noticed her literally *checking him out.*

"No, nothing," he said before answering his cellphone. She

watched him for a minute longer and then made her way to the bathroom, needing to wash her face. She was suddenly *very, very hot...*

CHAPTER TWO

She caught her reflection in the mirror. Her makeup was still perfect, her hair neatly in place. But she had a slight blush, the subtlest hint that Dean had gotten under her skin. He always did, actually, from the first day she worked for him. She knew that this was just a mild crush, though, just a little harmless infatuation. They were so far out of each other's leagues that even to entertain the thought would have been stupid.

He warmed her in the places he really shouldn't, though, and she found herself feeling for her warm wetness under her skirt. She figured she had a moment before they were airborne again, and she couldn't resist the urge.

Raquel closed her eyes, not wanting to see her reflection as she touched herself. She was a little embarrassed by the effect that her boss had on her. Her fingers teased over her panties, hinting at her intention to get *intimate* with herself. She was in no hurry, despite knowing that she was occupying the only bathroom on the plane.

The longest of moments passed, her fingers still just touching the surface of her panties. She wasn't pressing into herself as much as she was just dragging her fingers over herself from side to side. There was something delicious and decadent about this moment; something distinctly *woke* about the way she touched herself.

A light trickle seeped out of her, and she moaned, softly, still keenly aware of where she was. She pressed harder into herself, against herself, before pulling her panties to the side and touching herself directly. This was much better.

Her lips were full, *ready*, and soon enough, her finger was moving not just over her, but ever so slightly inside her. It went in easily, and she squeezed herself over the single-digit darting in and out of her now.

A knock on the door brought the moment to an abrupt end! She couldn't respond, not yet. She steadied herself, took a deep breath, removed her finger from herself.

"Just a moment," she said, before flushing the toilet and washing her hands. She pulled herself together and opened the door, coming face to face with Dean.

"I'm sorry, " she said, exiting the tiny cubicle.

"Don't be," he said, giving her the space she needed to leave.

Inside the bathroom, Dean looked at himself in the mirror as he took his thick shaft out of his trousers to pee. It was semi-hard, which surprised him. He hadn't thought of sex all day, except for that two-minute conversation with Luke earlier. Yes, Raquel was very attractive, and yes, the stewardess uniform made her look quite *fuckable,* but she was what, 21 or 22, and she wouldn't even look at him like that, he thought.

Just thinking of her now, though, was more than a little appetizing, made him a little hard. After he was done peeing, he found that his hand lingered on his lengthening shaft. He moved his thick fingers up and down on himself, thinking of Raquel but not really. If he wanted her, he wondered, what were the chances of him actually having her? This was just a passing thought, though, and after tugging on his *totem* a little while longer, he put it away, washed his hands, and exited the cubicle.

"You don't want to stretch your legs," Dean asked Raquel when he passed her. "It's going to be a long flight to Paris."

"I'm fine, thank you..." she said, before asking, "Do you know how much longer it will be before we take off again?"

"I can find out. But I think they'll just be guessing anyway...This plane needs to be upgraded, I think."

Raquel was staring at Dean again, unable to move her eyes from him even when it was clear that he was done speaking. He was staring too, and so, for the moment at least, this staring seemed appropriate.

"Sit...have a drink with me," Dean said.

"I don't drink," Raquel said, a little thrown by the request, but also realizing that her response was rude and dismissive.

"Alright then, sit and chat with me. We're going to be here for a while anyway..."

She sat down opposite him and crossed her legs. His eyes followed the movement, settled on her knee, then her thigh. He licked his lips, unintentionally, and certainly not meaning it in that creepy, desperate kind of way that Luke might have done. His lips were just dry.

There was a bit of a long silence between them, but it wasn't uncomfortable. She liked the way Dean was looking at her, and Dean liked the fact that she liked it. It meant that, if nothing else, she wasn't completely repulsed by him.

She had no reason to be, though. Dean was, by any standards, quite the catch. He'd been voted the *most eligible bachelor* three years in a row now, by some or other voting system organized by Manhattan's elite. He was balding but clean-shaven, so it didn't show. He had the most incredible gray eyes and a remarkably handsome face. He was also exceptionally well-built.

Raquel was also quite the sight. She was tiny, but her proportions were perfect. Add to this, her blonde hair and incredibly blue eyes, and she really was quite desirable. And then, of course, there was the uniform she had on, the skirt just the right length to reveal most of her upper thigh, the shirt revealing just the right amount of cleavage. She looked like an augmented version of an air hostess, a *caricature* of sorts. She looked like a beautiful exotic dancer in costume.

"You said earlier that you didn't like flying," Dean said, asking a question without a question mark.

"I just don't like things that I can't control," she said, her own eyes on the large bulge forming in the front of Dean's trousers. It was noticeable even though his legs were partly crossed in that way that men do, with his foot resting on the opposite knee.

"So you like being in control..." Another question *sans* question mark.

"I prefer it..." was her candid response.

He let this simmer in his head for a minute. He would love to be controlled by her. Or better yet, he would love to control her while giving her the impression that she was in control. That would be fun, he thought.

"Do you ever let yourself do anything, impulsive?" he asked.

"Sometimes, not often... And you?"

"Depends on your definition of *impulsive*..." he answered.

"What was the definition when you asked me?"q

Dean was quiet again, taking in the beauty in front of him. She was witty, which he liked. She wasn't nervous around him too, which he also liked. Raquel looked at him too, not really expecting an answer to the question but hoping that one would be forthcoming anyway.

"Well, let's just say that we could be here ten minutes or an hour, and we could pass the time a little better..."

She knew exactly what he meant. Or rather, she secretly hoped she did. There was something about Dean that she found *desperately* attractive, and she knew that if he wanted to, he could definitely *get it*. For the billionaire, she would give it up.

"I'm not sure you could handle passing the time a little better...with me..." she said.

"Why do you say that?"

"Well, you said it yourself... You're *old*!"

"Touché," he said, his interest definitely piqued.

Simon, another executive, was suddenly on the plane with them. They didn't hear him come in, so captivating was the exchange. "We'll be here for an hour, maybe two... Just came to get some beers!"

CHAPTER THREE

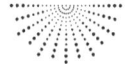

"So, we've got an hour..." Dean said, as a matter of fact.

"Maybe two," Raquel corrected.

"Maybe two..." Dean made this statement sound like a question.

Dean took a long sip of his drink, finishing it in a steady swig. He pulled the tray closer to him and opened the sliding side panel. "Let's see what we have here..." He took out an apple juice and handed it to Raquel, before taking out a beer for himself.

"You never struck me as a beer drinker," she said.

"You never struck me as a non-drinker!"

She raised her juice to him.

They sat for a minute, sipping their individual drinks. They made no secret of the fact that they were sizing each other up. There was no room for coy, not now. Somehow they knew, the both of them, that that particular ship had sailed when Raquel sat down for a *chat*.

Dean finished his beer first. He was tapping his bottom lip with his middle finger, contemplating his next move. If he was reading this wrong, it could be very embarrassing. If he was reading it right, this was about to be a whole lot more fun. Which one it was was the question.

He watched her for the briefest of moments. Then he stood up and walked to the bathroom. He went in, leaving the door ever so slightly ajar. And then, then he waited...

It was the longest thirty seconds of his life, but Dean let out a very loud sigh of relief when Raquel pushed the door open and slipped inside. She leaned against the door after she had pulled it shut and locked it. The ball, now, was in the billionaire's court.

Dean stepped forward so that he was towering over her and pressing her against the door with himself. His hands moved up and down her thighs slowly like he were a doctor feeling for an anomaly on her thighs. He was careful not to wrinkle her skirt. Raquel appreciated this.

He bent down to kiss her, the connection between their mouths, *fire*. His hands had moved so high up under her skirt that if he wanted to, he could pull her panties down. He really wanted to pull her panties down. He didn't, though, sending his thick, hot tongue into her mouth and letting her do what she wanted with it.

She hung on his neck as he lifted her off the ground, and settled her, seated, on the sink counter. Their mouths still joined, he found the zipper on the side of her skirt, and without looking, pulled it down and freed her of this fabric. He placed it carefully on the side of the sink opposite them, so as not to disturb it. Then he made quick work of her blouse buttons, placing the blouse atop the skirt.

"There, that's better..." he said.

"Better for who," she asked, bringing herself off the counter and turning so that Dean was now against the sink. She got on her knees and went to work on his belt, then his zipper. His trousers dropped immediately to his ankles. He struggled a bit but managed to remove them without removing his shoes. He unbuttoned and removed his own shirt.

All their clothes were now in as neat a pile as possible in the far corner, safely out of reach.

Dean again lifted Raquel up and turned so that again she was sitting on the counter. Again he was kissing her, his hands again moving up and down her thighs in a slow, deliberate rhythm. Then he was kissing her neck, his hands moving up and down on her back. He undid the clasp keeping her bra on her breasts and helped her out of it. Then he took her nipples, one at a time, between his full hot lips.

He wasn't sucking, but he also wasn't not. He just played with her nipples between his lips. Then he was flicking his tongue, still over just the nipple, *fast, furious, fire.* She felt what he was doing on her breasts *in her loins*. She desperately wanted to be out if her panties, with Dean doing what he was up top down below. Raquel did not have to wait long.

"You won't be needing these," he said as he pulled her panties the short distance from her hips to her ankles. He let her underwear fall to the floor, slid her towards him on the counter, moved back a little, and then brought his face square with her *dripping* place. And she really was dripping, so that for a good five or ten minutes all he was doing was licking the steady stream trickling out of her. His tongue made contact with her lips in much the same way her fingers had, and this surprised her. She had always thought the way she touched herself was unique to her, and then boom, Dean's tongue happened.

He licked her for as long as it took her to have a mild orgasm, and then, without warning, his tongue was inside her. She gasped, and then held onto his head hard, tried to push him away. It was intense, almost too intense, and she didn't know what to do with herself. The control freak in her didn't like this one bit.

He fought against her resistance successfully. He managed to get his thick tongue deep inside her, linger, and then pull another mild orgasm from her. If he wanted to, if it was his intention, there would be nothing mild about her orgasms. She knew this, and so it was a matter of paramount importance that she freed herself of him. She, too, had a skill that involved her mouth, and it was time to flip the script on this man who seemed determined to subdue her.

CHAPTER FOUR

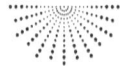

*S*he moaned loudly, distracting Dean just long
enough for her to push him off her and herself off
the counter. There wasn't a lot of room to move, so as soon
as her feet hit the floor, she pushed him against the wall
opposite and went down on her knees. She pulled his cotton
boxers down to his knees, and for the first time, came face to
face with his *pride*.

Raquel used both hands to hold the thick meat steady so
that she could slide her mouth over his clean head. Her
mouth fit comfortably, but she knew the length would be
challenging. She'd never had a very good gag reflex, so she
perfected other skills that didn't involve the entire length of
any man's shaft hitting the back of her throat.

She sucked on just his head for a long time. The sensation
was unfamiliar at first, and only when she took two and then
three inches of him into her wet mouth did it feel right, for
just a second. No sooner had he adjusted to this feeling, and
her tongue was flicking around just his head in complete
circles.

Then she was licking his entire shaft. The whole surface

of her tongue was on every part of his long, thickness. She licked hard, sent pulses through the hard penis that wanted nothing more than to be inside her. Her tongue was suddenly on his massive balls, licking, nibbling, biting. Dean lost his mind when, one by one, his nuts disappeared into Raquel's mouth and just stayed there.

She used every part of her mouth on Dean's nuts, applying different pressures and intensities with the various parts that made up her mouth. It was incredible, even more, incredible than her tongue had been on his shaft. No sooner had he settled into *this* sensation, and her mouth was wrapped around his head again, sucking hard on just the first few inches.

"Wait...wait..." he said, feeling like he was about to blow prematurely.

Raquel smiled to herself, sucked a little more before freeing him completely from her mouth. He pulled her up off the floor and kissed her hard. She kissed him back. They stood there kissing for a while, Dean's throbbing manhood brushing menacingly over her belly, just because of their height difference.

He turned her over, *bent her over* the sink. Then he got down on his knees, parted her legs. His tongue found her moist spot again, but this time there was no gingerly licking. His tongue went in deep and hard, and he pulled tremors from her that were not unlike an orgasm. She just held on to the sink, braced herself against the assault.

She wanted to feel him inside her now, all of him, but Dean was not quite done yet. He parted her ass cheeks, and after wetting his index finger with his own saliva, tapped the rosebud over and over again. It bloomed to magnificent life. His tongue was back inside her, and moments later, the finger was slipping into her other *happy place*.

His finger went as deep as his tongue was. It was an

incredible feeling, and Raquel found herself submitting, much against her will. She was settling into being pleased by the man she had secretly had a crush on for a while. She closed her eyes and exhaled hard when the finger was no longer inside her.

This absence wasn't for long, though. But this time, his tongue was where his finger just was, his finger replacing his tongue in her front. How he was managing this in his *crouching tiger* position on the floor was a testament, if nothing else, to his agility.

CHAPTER FIVE

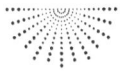

*T*he knock on the door was unexpected. It was loud and intrusive and very *Luke*. It wasn't, though.

"The mechanics want a word," came Simon's voice from the other side.

"Just a second..." Dean said, before returning his tongue to Raquel's beautiful bud. She let him continue for a while but then realized that Dean's meeting with the mechanics was probably the only thing keeping them from taking off.

"You should go... We can continue this later..." she said.

After another minute, Dean saw her point and pulled himself from her. He put his clothes back on, needing to take his shoes off this time to make it possible. Raquel just stood against the sink, watching him try in vain to rinse the flush from his face. She locked herself in the bathroom after Dean had left.

She looked at herself in the mirror. Laughing at the *flush* on Dean was a bit hypocritical because she was just as disheveled. She took her hair out of its bun and tied it again in a looser version of its previous self. She looked at her body, still naked, and couldn't believe what had just happened. She wasn't sure who had seduced whom, but that really didn't matter now.

Raquel found her hands exploring her full lips once more. She couldn't resist. She couldn't help herself. She didn't know what the mechanics had to say to the owner of the jet that they couldn't share with the pilot, so just in case they were minutes from take-off, she decided to put these few minutes to good use.

Leaning back against the door, much like she was the first time, except that this time she was completely naked. Her finger moved over her, side to side, and then in small circles. She too was in no hurry, even though, in the back of her mind, she kept expecting the plane's engines to start up.

Another knock. Another interruption.

"You gonna be much longer?" This time it *was* Luke.

"A minute..." She was determined to see herself through to the end, no matter what Luke needed the bathroom for.

In the end, all the distractions took their toll. Three times she tried to bring herself to a quick orgasm, and three times she failed. She just got dressed and pulled herself together as best she could. Then, taking a final moment for composure, she opened the door.

Luke was still standing in the door. He looked like he had no intention of moving either. So they just stood there, a strange stalemate, for what seemed like forever. She asked him to move, with just her eyes. He answered, *no*, with just his. She laughed. He licked his lips.

He could not be serious, she thought.

Another long moment passed between them, and eventually, Luke gave way, enough for Raquel to move out of the cubicle, but not enough for her not to rub up against him as she did.

"We've still got Paris," he said.

"No, we really don't!" She answered sternly for the first time.

He just looked at her like he really thought they did...

CHAPTER SIX

*D*ean's phone was ringing as soon as he walked back onto the plane. He looked at Raquel; half nodded into his phone before saying, 'hello!'

She left the plane, needing the distraction from her very pressing need to climax.

She walked down the stairs, onto the hanger's concrete floor. She greeted the mechanics and then walked to where the passengers in her care were seated, still drinking beer. Luke would probably join them soon, she knew, but this didn't matter. All she needed to do was flirt with one or two of the others, which should, technically, convince him once and for all of her disinterest.

Raquel learned that the five men were Simon, Garth, two Jim's, and Roderick. They all served in various executive capacities at the *Cane Corporation*, marketing, finance, operations, legal and public relations. And it was clear that they all really loved their jobs. They also had nothing but praise for Dean, who was both chairman of the board and CEO, not a common combination. She could tell that this wasn't fake praise, either. It was borne of genuine respect.

The youngest, based purely on his appearance, was Garth. He was also the least attractive. The VP in charge of marketing had that *just out of college too many sleepless nights* look about him. So he looked tired but wired on caffeine and *red bull*. He wasn't the best option, therefore, to make Luke feel any sort of way because Luke was miles more attractive than Garth, and a whole lot more confident. The best option, for this particular purpose, was Roderick.

Roderick was calm and collected. He had that quiet confidence that said he had nothing to prove. He wasn't good looking. He was great looking. He was the best looking of the bunch, including Dean. Roderick was also the tallest, taller than Luke by at least half a foot, making him a mammoth of a man.

Raquel wasn't sure about the depth of Luke's Napoleon Complex. But she did know that men were as visual as women, maybe more so, when it came to the comparisons they drew with one another. She looked at Roderick, who was also looking at her. She smiled, held his gaze just a moment too long, and then turned away and back into the conversation the others were having.

"We'll be airborne within the hour," a voice said behind them. They turned to see Luke walk towards them, followed by Dean, who had delivered the feedback.

"I'll let Paris know," Simon said.

"I already have," Dean said, taking a beer from Roderick and positioning himself between the *giant* and Raquel.

"So, Raquel, beer?" Roderick asked.

"She doesn't drink..." Dean answered for her.

All of the men looked around at one another, then at Dean. Both Jims' smirked. Luke laughed loudly. Simon just looked away in that way that said he knew something the rest of them did not.

Raquel thought of how to save the situation, but couldn't

for the moment. Roderick and Dean were sizing each other up. There had always been a playful competition between them and now wouldn't be any different, it seemed.

There was nothing to it now. Raquel and Roderick flirted openly, and Dean, playfully, laid claim to her. The tug of war between them was really just light fun. Dean took it seriously, though, at times, more than he should. Roderick was very deliberate in his efforts to rub Dean up the wrong way. They morphed from serious to playful and back to serious again. Raquel relished the attention.

"So, out of all of us, who *would* you sleep with?" Jim St. John asked. He'd been quiet for the most part, so that he asked this question surprised everyone.

"In order of preference," Roderick said, a cheeky slant to his voice.

Raquel looked at all of them. She walked around, checking all of them out now, really checking them out. This was the first time she could really look at them freely, uninhibited. She took her time, made them squirm.

Then, quite frankly, she said, "I'm not playing this game!"

She walked back towards the plane with every eye in the hanger on her. The mechanics also stopped working, caught in a moment, not seeing too many beautiful women on a normal workday. The pilot had also just walked into the hanger, having just finished up with air traffic control. He went up to the mechanics to chat quickly, the not so routine maintenance almost done.

Raquel walked into the aircraft and checked her trolley. She replenished what needed replenishing and locked the cart in place. Then she sat in her seat, checked her messages, and fixed her face, again unnecessarily.

"You do realize that you really don't need that, right..." Dean said, catching her off guard.

"I do..."

"You really had a field day with that little game outside, didn't you?" He was really fishing for an answer to the question the *other* Jim posed, mildly curious.

"No... I did not... It was a little awkward..." She answered, honestly.

"So, if you had to pick..." Dean asked her outright.

"I'm not sure," she said.

He went to his seat. He started to go through paperwork, but not really. He was after a definitive answer, part ego, part something else. She seemed determined not to give him the answer he sought. And he seemed to have given up.

He really hadn't.

Raquel watched him *work*. She watched him move a pen across many pages, too quickly. Nobody read that fast. Not even Dean Cane. She knew that this was a rouse, and she wanted it to end one way.

Dean wasn't aware of the game she was playing. He couldn't comprehend how he, as suave and successful as he was, would ever be played. So this didn't register as a possibility.

But play him she had. And she was not done yet. When she had said earlier that she hated things and situations she couldn't control, she was not lying. They made her very uncomfortable. Now that she had taken full control over whatever this thing between her and her billionaire boss was, it would be easier for her to give him a little back.

Just a little.

Raquel stood up and went to the bathroom. She entered, left the door ever so slightly ajar, and waited. It was the longest thirty seconds of her life, when suddenly and without warning the door swung open, and it was Dean who locked it behind himself this time...

CHAPTER SEVEN

*T*he two of them stood in place and, for a moment, quietly just looked at each other. Raquel started to take her own blouse off, Dean doing the same with his shirt. She took her skirt off; he did the same to his shoes and trousers. She took her bra off, and they both removed their panties and boxers, respectively.

All the clothing was stacked in the same neat pile as before.

"So, we've got an hour..." Dean said.

"No, we really don't," Raquel said, turning towards the sink, leaning on the counter, and watching him behind her in the mirror.

He came up behind her, pressed his fast forming erection against her butt-cheeks, and ran just the tips of his fingers up and down he back. She arched leaned back, and Dean brought his mouth down to hers so that they were kissing.

He bent his knees, tucked himself between legs, holding his heavy erection in his hand so as to direct it. Dean held his meat, took aim, and with one hand on Raquel's hip, he brought her back just enough for his head to make contact with the part of her he was gunning for.

"Slowly, " she said, nervous suddenly.

"Relax, no rush..."

He pulled on her hip a little more, straightened his legs just a little so that his whole head was snug inside her. He let go of her hip, now and stayed motionless. If this was going to happen now, if it was going to happen fast, then she would have to feed herself with him. So, again, control was back with Raquel.

He leaned with his back against the wall, careful not to remove himself from Raquel, who was only just getting comfortable with the mushroom plugging her hole. She went back with him, stopping only when he did. She placed her hands on the counter, dug deep with her fingers, and pushed, forcing inch after massive inch into her. Dean watched as half, and then two-thirds of him disappeared inside her. She took more than he thought she'd be able to.

The female body really was full of wonder and mystery, Dean thought.

He watched as she pulled herself off him until just his head was inside her, then ease back down until the two-thirds were once again parked in place. He enjoyed watching her work as much as he enjoyed the feeling of her work. He thought, for the briefest moment, that if he just stood up, he would get all of himself inside her and be done with it, but he didn't.

This was more than he expected, more than he thought he was going to get.

She moved a little too far, and all of Dean was outside of her. He stood up straight, stepped forward, turned her around, and lifted her onto the counter. He stepped forward one more step, pulled her closer to him, and pointed his penis back towards the place it just was.

He was in, both their eyes on where their bodies now met. Dean now held on to the counter and dug into her with just half of himself for a while. Then he achieved the two thirds and settled into comfortable, easy strokes. Raquel was nervous, feeling the threat of *more* with each stroke, scared that he would put all of his thickness inside her and break her in half.

He didn't, though. He was uncomfortably big, but overall he was gentle. He also had such control of himself that she found that she really trusted him, trusted that he wouldn't do anything that might cause her permanent harm. He was kissing her now, an attempt at distracting her from what he wasn't trying to do.

Another inch inside her and she couldn't kiss him back. She couldn't breathe. She couldn't move.

Dean was almost all the way inside her. He could feel it. Just a few more strokes and he would be home, completely, all in. He was more careful now, more considerate. He paid attention to her every response, needing to read her responses just right so that his own were appropriate.

They were both deathly silent, so quiet that they could both hear, quite clearly, the order in which the others got on the plane. Luke was asking, loudly, where Dean and Raquel were. Simon, as loudly, told him to get over himself. It was so quiet in the bathroom that they both heard, quite clearly, every single one of their seatbelts being clasped.

Dean placed both hands on Raquel's butt and pulled her towards him, moving himself the inch and a half towards her to gain, at last, full entry. The sensation was incredible, but there was no time to savor it. She needed to climax. He really needed to climax. And they both needed to get back to the others who knew, obviously, exactly what was going on behind the closed - and locked - door.

Raquel was taking him, easier and easier with each full

entry. Dean was going harder with each stroke. They were both becoming more animated now, making a series of sounds that let everyone who cared to listen now that they were both incredibly, incredibly close.

Raquel wasn't as close as Dean, though, but there was no way for Dean to know this. He was pumping so hard into her that even when be started cumming, all she could process was the power with which his penis was pounding away at her depths. He came hard, and he came aplenty, but then he was spent, unable to move.

Raquel needed him to remain hard just a moment longer, just a few minutes. She was so close to climax she could smell it. She threw her hands around his neck, lifting herself off the counter. Dean stumbled back against the wall. She was moving herself up and down on him as he held her up and in place. She had to *fuck herself* to climax, but this wasn't a problem. Dean provided the perfect body to do it with.

She let him leave the bathroom first, wanting him to get the brunt of it. Many minutes later, she exited, going straight for the trolley, walking down the aisle to distribute drinks. Out of the corner of her eye, through the window, she saw clouds. She wondered how long they had been airborne.

Luke looked disappointed. She smiled at him, handing him a drink. Then, turning to Dean, she asked, "Will you be needing me in Paris, Sir?"

"Oh, you know I will..."

ABOUT THE AUTHOR

Tala Melton is an emerging erotica author of naughty maids and their billionaire bosses.

Readers: I want to expand a few of the stories to see where the characters can be explored further. If there are any of the stories that you would like to read more about again, I'd love to hear from you!

Visit my blog at Tala Melton Blog
Join my newsletter for free exclusive previews Tala Melton Newsletter
Follow me on Twitter at Tala Melton Twitter
Like my page on Facebook at Tala Melton FB

Sign up for Free Stories from Xplicit Press Authors
Xplicit Press Updates
Like Xplicit Press on Facebook
Follow Xplicit Press on Twitter

MORE NAUGHTY MAID STORIES BY TALA MELTON

Naughty Maids and The Dirty Billionaire Bosses

www.ingramcontent.com/pod-product-compliance
Lightning Source LLC
Chambersburg PA
CBHW020813130626
46554CB00006B/2422